To Carme Solé Vendrell
and the mountain

Copyright © David McKee 1985, 2005
The rights of David McKee to be identified as the author and
illustrator of this work have been asserted by him in accordance
with the Copyright, Designs and Patents Act, 1988.
This mini edition first published by Andersen Press in 2005.
First published in Great Britain in 1985 by Andersen Press Ltd.,
20 Vauxhall Bridge Road, London SW1V 2SA.
Published in Australia by Random House Australia Pty.,
20 Alfred Street, Milsons Point, Sydney, NSW 2061.
Colour separated in Switzerland by Photolitho AG, Zürich.
Printed and bound in Singapore by Tien Wah Press.

10   9   8   7   6   5   4   3   2   1

British Library Cataloguing in Publication Data available.

ISBN 1 84270 548 2

This paper is made from wood pulp from sustainable forests

TWO MONSTERS

David McKee

Andersen Press
London

There was once a monster that lived quietly on the west side of the mountain.

On the east side of the mountain lived another monster.

Sometimes the monsters spoke together
through a hole in the mountain.

But they never *saw* each other.

One evening the first monster called through
the hole, "Can you see how beautiful it is?
Day is departing?"

"Day departing?" called back the second
monster. "You mean night arriving, you twit!"

"Don't call me a twit, you dumbo, or I'll get angry," fumed the first monster and he felt so annoyed that he could hardly sleep.

The other monster felt just as irritated and he *slept* very *badly* as *well*.

The next morning the first monster felt awful after such a bad night. He shouted through the hole, "Wake up, you numskull, night is leaving."

"Don't be stupid, you peabrain!" answered
the second. "That is day arriving."
And with that he picked up a stone and
threw it over the mountain.

"Rotten shot, you fat ignoramus!" called the
first monster as the stone missed him. He
picked up a bigger stone and hurled it back

That stone also missed. "Hopeless, you hairy, long-nosed nerk!" howled the second monster, and he threw back a rock which knocked the top off the mountain.

"You're just a stupid old wind-filled prune!" shouted the first monster as he heaved a boulder that knocked another piece off the mountain.

And you're a bandy-legged, soggy cornflake!"
replied the second monster. This time he
kicked a huge rock just for a change.

As the day passed the rocks grew bigger and bigger and the insults grew longer and longer.

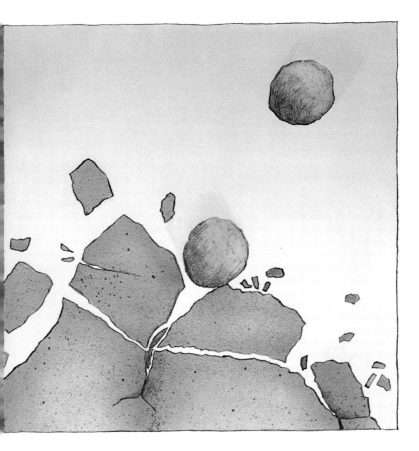

Both of the monsters remained untouched but the mountain was being knocked to pieces.

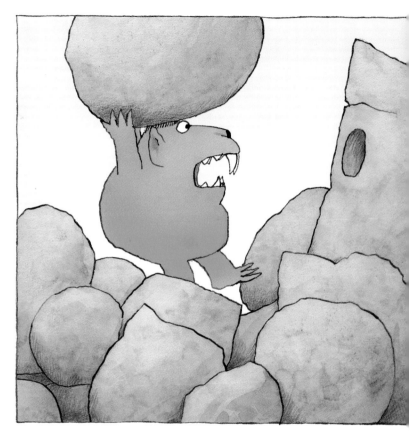

"You're a hairy, overstuffed, empty-headed, boss-eyed mess!" shouted the first monster as he threw yet another massive boulder.

"You're a pathetic, addlebrained, smelly, lily-livered custard tart!" screamed the second monster hurling a yet larger rock.

That rock finally smashed the last of the mountain and for the very first time the monsters saw each other.

This happened just at the beginning of another sunset.

"Incredible," said the first monster putting
down the rock he was holding.
"There's night arriving. You were right."

"Amazing," gasped the second monster dropping his boulder.
"You are right, it is day leaving."

They walked to the middle of the mess they had made to watch the arrival of the night and the departure of the day together.

"That was rather fun," giggled the first monster. "Yes, wasn't it," chuckled the second. "Pity about the mountain."